WEBSTER
THE SCAREDY SPIDER

Also Available

Board Books:
Hermie: A Common Caterpillar
Flo the Lyin' Fly
Webster the Scaredy Spider

Picture Books:
Hermie: A Common Caterpillar
Flo the Lyin' Fly

MAX LUCADO'S

Hermie & Friends™

WEBSTER
THE SCAREDY SPIDER

Story by Troy Schmidt
Illustrations by GlueWorks Animation
Based on the characters from Max Lucado's
Hermie: A Common Caterpillar

CANDLE BOOKS

Published in the UK in 2005 by Candle Books (a publishing imprint of Lion Hudson plc).

Distributed by Marston Book Services Ltd, PO Box 269, Abingdon, Oxon OX14 4YN

Text and art copyright © 2004 by Max Lucado.
Story by Troy Schmidt, based on the characters from Max Lucado's *Hermie: A Common Caterpillar*.
Illustrations by GlueWorks Animation.

Published in Nashville, Tennessee, by Tommy Nelson®, a Division of Thomas Nelson, Inc.

Scripture quotations in this book are from the *International Children's Bible®, New Century Version®*, © 1986, 1988, 1999 by Tommy Nelson®, a Division of Thomas Nelson, Inc. All rights reserved.

Worldwide co-edition organised and produced by Lion Hudson plc,
Mayfield House, 256 Banbury Road, Oxford, OX2 7DH, England.
Tel: +44 (0) 1865 302750   Fax: +44 (0) 1865 302757
Email: coed@lionhudson.com
www.lionhudson.com

Printed in Singapore

"Don't worry, because I am with you.
Don't be afraid, because I am your God.
I will make you strong and will help you. . . ."
– Isaiah 41:10

It was a stormy day in the garden. Lightning flashed. Thunder cracked. But the ladybird twins and their mother, Lucy Ladybird, were not scared.

"I'm the bravest ever," boasted Hailey.

"I'm the bravest ever, ever, ever," bragged Bailey.

Suddenly, Lucy saw the scariest thing a ladybird could see . . . a big, scary spider!

"Run for your ladybird lives!" Lucy shouted. And they did.

If they had stayed, they would have seen that it was a big, scary shadow of a not-so-big-and-scary spider.

It was Webster. A small, young spider on holiday. Webster was very smart and liked to use big words.

"What an agreeable, amiable, pleasurable day," said Webster as the sun came out. He jumped to the ground.

"Where is everyone? All I see is a – **LEAF!**"

Webster was very afraid of leaves.

"It's okay," he told himself. "It's not like it's a – **STICK!**"

Webster was even more afraid of sticks.

"Why am I so afraid of everything?" Webster said to himself.

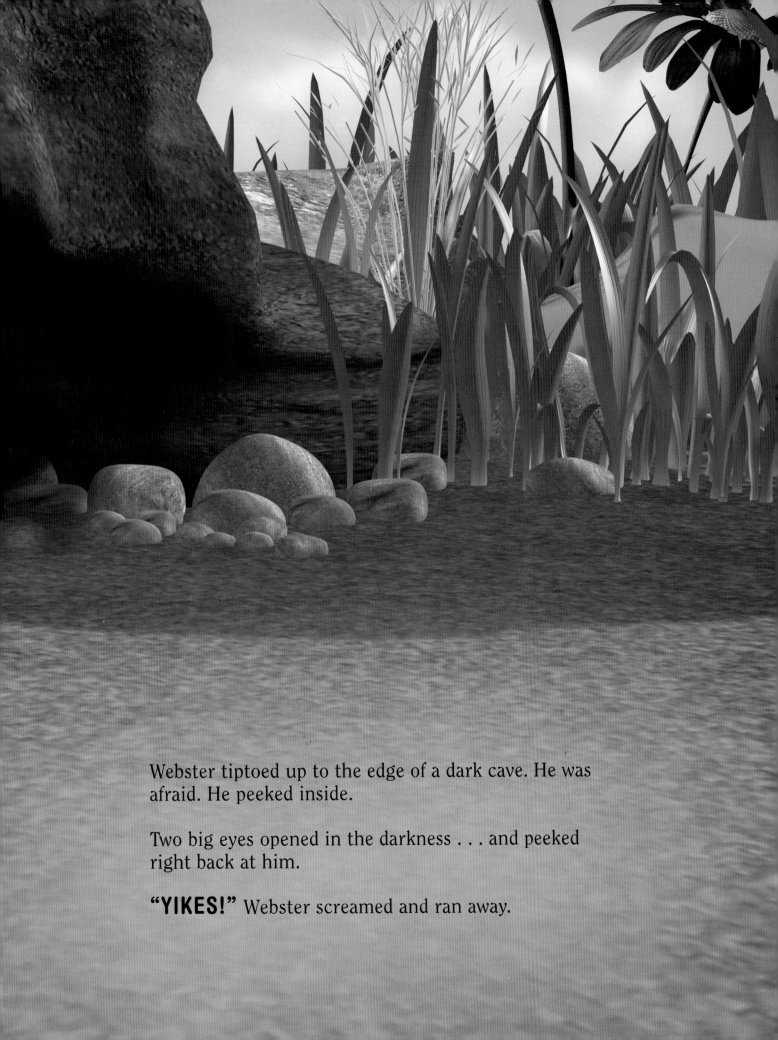

Webster tiptoed up to the edge of a dark cave. He was afraid. He peeked inside.

Two big eyes opened in the darkness . . . and peeked right back at him.

"YIKES!" Webster screamed and ran away.

Meanwhile, the ladybirds were still afraid and hurrying home. On the way, they saw Hermie the caterpillar.

"Run, Hermie, run! A spider is after us," Lucy shouted.

Hermie laughed. "There are no spiders in our garden."

But the ladybirds didn't listen and flew away.

"They are being so silly," Hermie said to himself.

"Excuse me," a voice said.

Hermie turned to see who was behind him.

"A SPIDER!" Hermie yelled.

"A CATERPILLAR!" Webster yelled.

Both were afraid. And both screamed, "AHHHHHHHHH!" as loud as they could for a very long time.

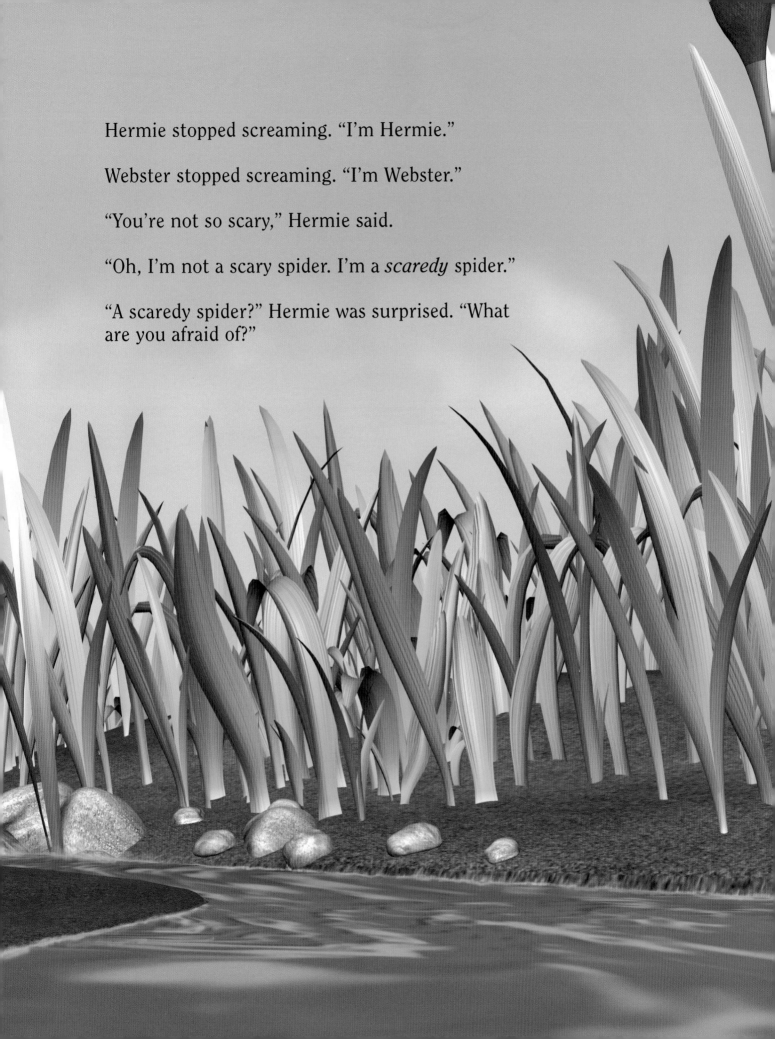

Hermie stopped screaming. "I'm Hermie."

Webster stopped screaming. "I'm Webster."

"You're not so scary," Hermie said.

"Oh, I'm not a scary spider. I'm a *scaredy* spider."

"A scaredy spider?" Hermie was surprised. "What are you afraid of?"

Webster started counting all the things that made him scared.

"Oh, I'm afraid of leaves, sticks, dark places, meeting new friends, lizards, water, heights, swinging through the air on my silk threads. Things like that."

"Come with me, Webster, and I'll show you how to be brave. I want you to meet my friends, too."

Webster was afraid but wanted to be brave, so he followed Hermie.

At Flo the fly's house, they also found Schneider Snail, Antonio Ant, and Wormie the caterpillar.

When Flo saw Webster she flew away.

When Schneider saw Webster he zoomed away.

When Antonio saw Webster he ran away.

Only Wormie stayed.

Webster asked Wormie, "How did you become so brave?"

"I know God is with me," Wormie said.

"God can help you be brave, too," Hermie said. "Right, God?"

"That's right, Hermie," God said. "Webster, you are safe with Me. I'm always with you, even when you are afraid."

Webster was too scared to listen. He ran away.

"Webster's going to need a friend to remind him that I love him," God said.

"I'll be his friend," Hermie promised.

Hermie found Webster. "Let's dress you like a ladybird. No one's afraid of a ladybird."

Webster agreed. But it didn't work.

When the ladybirds saw Webster, they screamed, **"A SPIDER!"** and ran away.

"I've got it!" Hermie said. "Let's plan a big concert starring you. Everyone loves a concert."

But it didn't work.

When the crowd saw Webster, they shrieked, **"A SPIDER!"** and ran away.

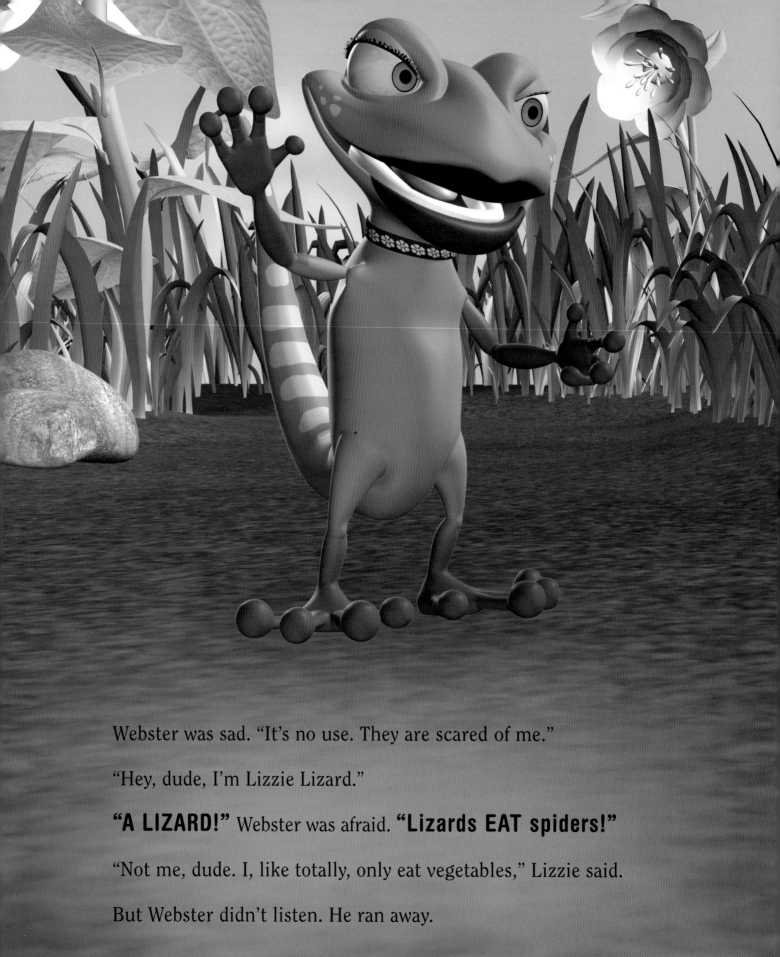

Webster was sad. "It's no use. They are scared of me."

"Hey, dude, I'm Lizzie Lizard."

"A LIZARD!" Webster was afraid. **"Lizards EAT spiders!"**

"Not me, dude. I, like totally, only eat vegetables," Lizzie said.

But Webster didn't listen. He ran away.

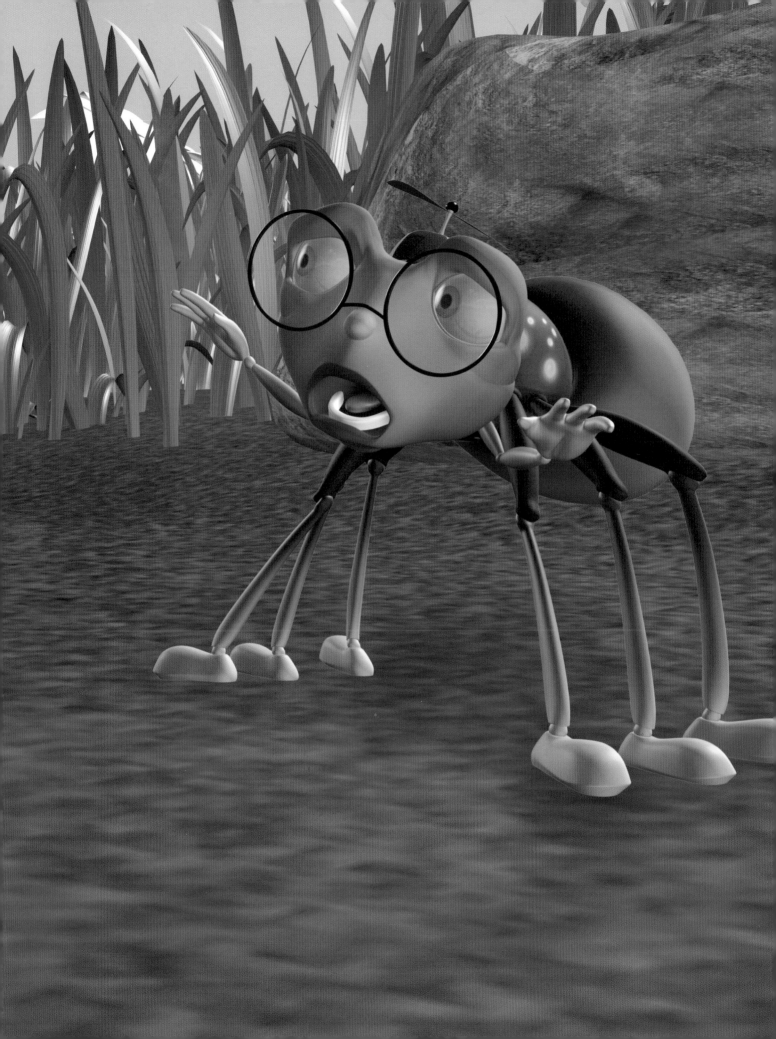

The garden buzzed with news of the spider.

"I'm afraid of spiders," said Flo the fly.

"Me, too!" said Schneider Snail.

"But Webster is a friendly spider," Hermie said.

"He's a scaredy spider, not a scary spider,"
Wormie said.

No one listened.

"A spider's a spider! Webster has to go!" said Milt
the caterpillar.

Hailey whispered to Bailey, "You know, Bailey, maybe Hermie and Wormie are right. We never really got a good look at Webster."

"You're right, Hailey. Let's go and see if Webster really is big and scary."

No one noticed when the twins left to look for Webster.

As the crowd went to tell Webster to leave, Hermie and Wormie prayed.

"God, what can we do to help Webster?"

"Be his friend," God said. "The others are scared of Webster. But because I am always with each of you, no one has to be afraid."

Hermie and Wormie were looking for Webster when they heard:

"MUM, HELP US!"

Everyone rushed to the river.

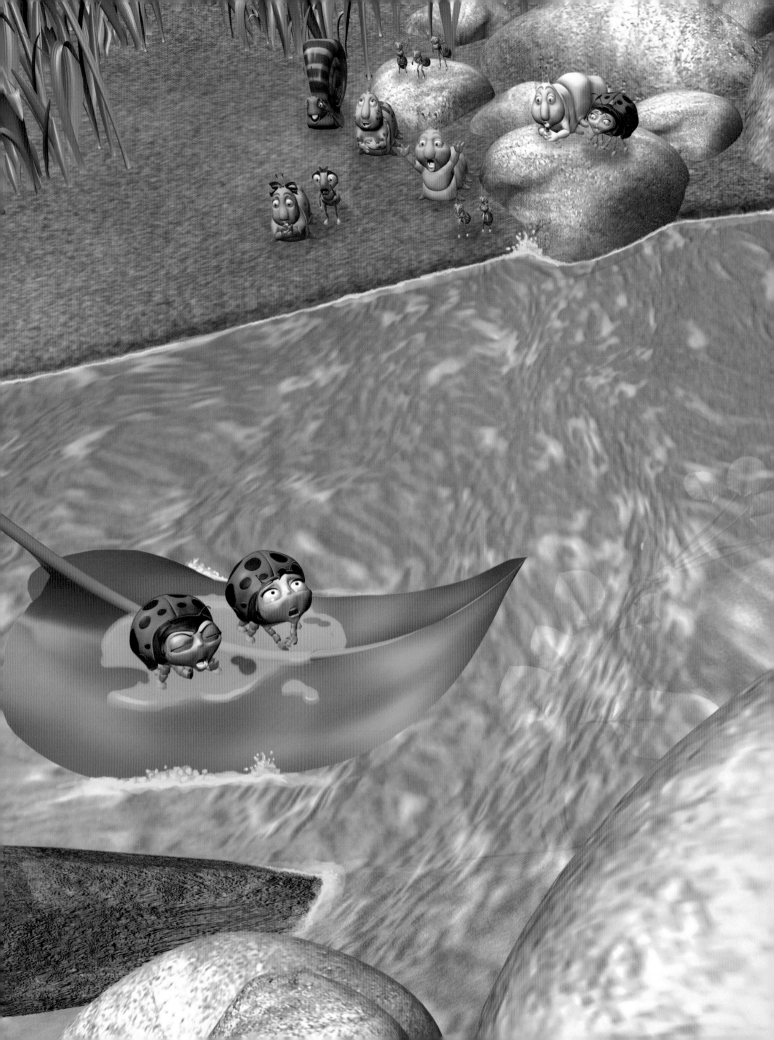

It was Hailey and Bailey. The twins were on a runaway leaf in the river and heading straight for a dangerous waterfall.

"FLY, LADYBIRDS, FLY!" Wormie said.

"We can't. We're stuck on this gooey, sticky leaf," said Hailey.

"SOMEBODY HELP US!" Bailey cried.

But no one could reach them. The leaf was moving too fast.

Webster wanted to help. He was afraid to pray, but he was more afraid for the ladybirds.

"What can I do, God?"

"You can help them, Webster," God said.

"Me?"

"Yes. Don't worry. I'll be with you."

For the first time, Webster felt brave.

Quickly, Webster spun a silk net to catch the runaway leaf.

Webster was not afraid.

Next, Webster swung to the leaf.

He pulled Hailey, then Bailey from the sticky goo.

The twins flew to safety, but now Webster was stuck.

"OH, NO!" The crowd gasped as the web broke. Webster and the leaf plunged over the waterfall.

"**LOOK!**" shouted Hailey and Bailey.

Swinging up from the waterfall was . . .

"WEBSTER!" the crowd cheered. As he landed safely, the crowd started singing:

"For he's a brave little spider,
For he's a brave little spider,
For he's a brave little spider,
Which everyone now likes!"

"My bravery came from God," Webster said.

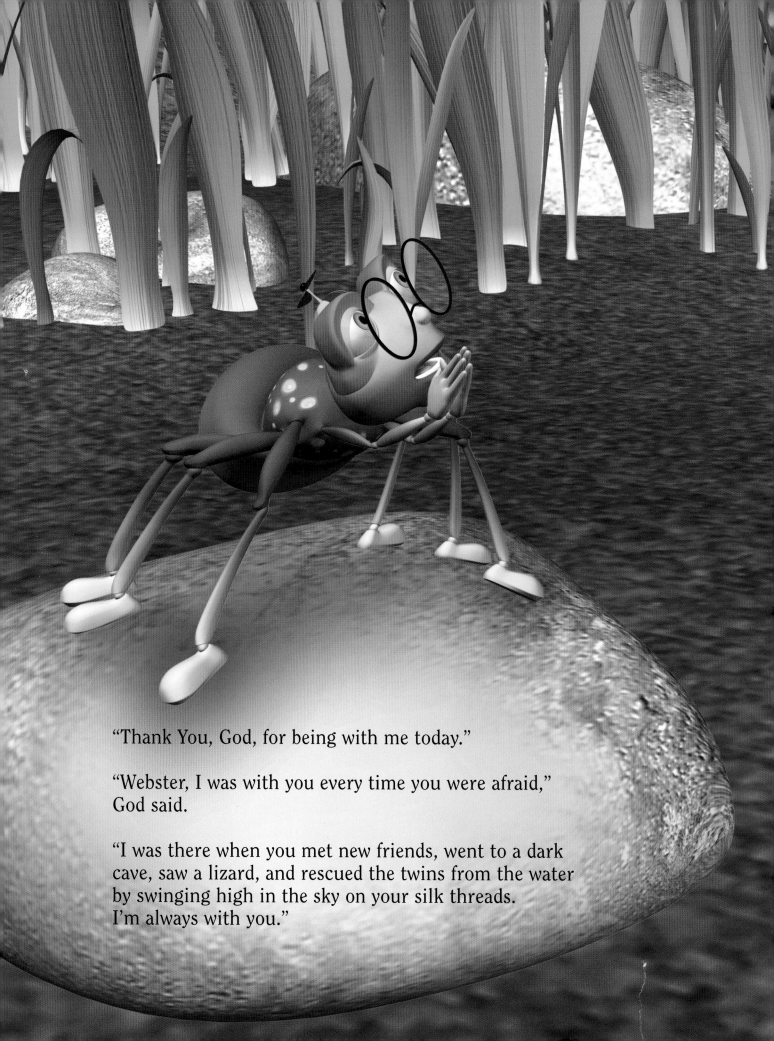

"Thank You, God, for being with me today."

"Webster, I was with you every time you were afraid,"
God said.

"I was there when you met new friends, went to a dark
cave, saw a lizard, and rescued the twins from the water
by swinging high in the sky on your silk threads.
I'm always with you."

From that day forward, Webster was no longer a scaredy spider. Soon he had many new friends. One was even a lizard named Lizzie. Whenever Webster was afraid, he remembered that God was with him. And that made Webster brave.